CONTENTS

This bit of nonsense was written for Aalst Magazine back in 2001. The magazine launched an international poetry competition, and it was one of those where you were given the title and left to get on with it. The fact that it won the Shoestring Award for best poem, I can only put down to the guess that I was the only one daft enough to write a poem entitled Chubby's Crematorium and Burger Bar.

Chubby's Crematorium and Burger Bar

The night was young, the moonlight shone

As I stood beneath the stars

And the smell of freshly roasted flesh

Wafted out from Chubby`s

Burger Bar

I drifted past the ash filled urns

And flowers `In memoria`

And other such respectful things

One finds at crematoria

I`d been there once before you see
Albeit in a different guise
In fact, it was quite recently
Just after my demise

I didn`t know of Chubby`s scam
Hadn`t figured the connection
Between his crematorium
And all-night food concession

But being dead gives one an edge
And heightens one`s perception
And the anger welled inside me
As I considered his deception

The urns I passed contained remains
Of people`s bones and ash
But Chubby kept the fleshy bits
To serve with chips or mash

I didn't live my life on earth
A good and honest worker
To end up in a shish kebab
Nor in a megaburger

And so, I'd come to settle scores
It got a little grubby
I'm sorry friend, it had to be
I had to kill off Chubby

I took him by his greasy hair
He began to make excuses
So, I boiled him in last night's fat
And stewed him in his juices

But that is all behind me now
And Chubs and I are partners
Dispensing all night take-aways
Up here in the hereafter

There may not be much substance

To our nouvelle haute cuisine

But ghosts eat very little

And they hate to cause a scene

The reason for their patronage

If only in a wry sense:

Next week we`re opening a bar

When we get our spirit license

Shoestring Award Winner 1st Place Aalst
Magazine Dec 2001

While we're on this somewhat macabre theme, here's another one, featuring those two notorious grave robbers, Burke and Hare.

Babe Ruth's Bat

On a night as dark as lead-blackened pitch

Messrs. Burke and Hare did ply their trade

Robbing the graves of the newly dead

And selling their bodies for £2 a head

Unbeknownst to them, on this evening in question

A twist in the laws of physics occurred

And from out of the future a casket arrived

With an American national hero inside

"That's not the coffin of Arthur McCrumb,"

Said Burke, who was six feet down in the hole

"It must be," said Hare. "It isn't, God's truth.

It says on the plate: 'Here lies Babe Ruth'."

They opened the casket and gazed at the corpse

Puzzled by all the weird clothes that he wore

"Good heavens," said Burke, "He's wearing a hat

and look, he's been buried with some sort of
bat."

They carried the casket, Babe Ruth and his bat

And took it to Fife railway station

Intending to send it as Glasgow bound freight

But the train was three days and four hours late.

"The train now arriving at farn forfar fee"

Said the station announcer in adenoidal grunts,

"Is the farfar from finfur and fellit-begdit,"

So, the pair dropped the casket and legged it."

"And that is the provenance of this baseball bat,"

Said the sly looking man at the jumble sale stall,

"And it's yours for only a fiver,"

Don't you believe him?

Didn't think that you would

I can tell you that I didn't either!

If poets wrote doggerel 1 (Hemans)

The boy stood on the burning deck

Whence all but he had fled

Never the brightest spark that lad

That's why he finished up dead

This one has a bit more of a serious theme and was inspired by a news item regarding twitchers driving the length and breadth of the country in order to tick a box with a bird's name next to it. For some obscure reason, it sounds best when read in a John Cooper-Clarke accent.

Petrel Crisis

The tanker rolls in on the incoming tide

The tug boats nestling by her side

To guide the wide leviathan

Conceived, constructed, crewed by man

And from her bilges oil gushes

Headlong into the sea it rushes

Droplets form and coalesce

To waste the watery wilderness

A stormy petrel rides the swell

Unfamiliar with the unctuous smell

Unaware of the danger it brings

As the silky slick enshrouds its wings

Whilst on the shore-line, looking out

An ornithologist almost shouts

With rage, with grief but he makes no sound

As he watches the petrel slowly drown

Choking back tears, he heads for home
In his wax polished car with gleaming chrome
He reflects on the scene, so savage and cruel
As he stops at a garage to fill up with fuel

The irony of conservation
A bird-watcher at a filling station
Making his personal contribution
To systematic sea pollution

As the tankers gush and the seabirds drown
We all add to the problem in litres and pounds
And baulk at the latest fuel price hike
Save the petrel........ride a bike.

Continuing with the theme of cars, this bit of doggerel came about when I was doing a brief stint as a taxi driver in Bournemouth, Dorset. As some of the town's little darlings couldn't be trusted to behave on school buses, the council forked out for them to travel in style by taxi. How we all used to love the school run (especially me, I drove a six-seater!). Getting anywhere near the school gates required nerves of steel:

The Montessori Rally

Up and down the country

On mock Tudor housing estates

The Suzukis and the Subarus

Are revving by the gates

In clouds of carbon monoxide

And other exhaust emissions

These giant people-carriers

Set out on their daily missions

The drivers: determined, ambitious

Nails polished, hair styled, lips glossed

And in the back of the roomy interior

Sits a four-year-old looking quite lost

The race lasts for only a mile
From home to school gates where it ends
But what is the point of a big, showy car
If you can't show it off to your friends?

So now we reach the finish line
The competition increases more
Who can find a parking space
Close to the school front door?

A Toyota stops in the bus only lane
The driver: intent she will win it
Throws on her hazard warning lights
To show that she'll 'just be a minute'.

And by the Montessori gate
The traffic forms a solid wedge
As a 4x4 tries a three point turn
And reverses into a hedge

The race is run ten thousand times
Twice daily, rain or shine
To get the nation's under fives
To school and home on time.

But tell me, where's the pleasure

In this high-pressure country of ours

In denying our children a good daily walk

By forcing them into our cars?

If poets wrote doggerel 2: (Burns)

Should old acquaintance be forgot

And never brought to mind?

I'll blame it on yon whiskey, dear;

And I'll ken your name next time

From children, we move to the subject of dogs.
For those of you who follow my <u>nature blogs</u> you
will know that I am often accompanied by my
partner 'The Intrepid Local Guide' and her
canine companion, 'Jack The Navigator Hound'.
This one is for Jack.

RUSSELLIAC

A friend asked me the other day

For the opposite of aphrodisiac

I answered him without delay

That the antonym was russelliac

For a Jack-in-the bed makes all hopes forlorn

When feelings are running tender and dear

When a sneezing, wheezing, snuffling yawn

Precedes a Jack Russell's nose in your ear.

I was originally going to publish this book of twaddle at the beginning of the century, for many of the poems were written in the late 1900s (how weird that sounds now), under the title 'What A Millenium That Was'. Twenty years later, and unfortunately, they all seem still topical.

Bob The Begging Dog

I'm Bob the begging dog
You've seen me on the street
Sitting outside of Sainsbury's
And getting under your feet

I don't belong to him y'know
He rents me by the day
Coz the more that you take pity on him
The more yer gonna pay

I've worked with all the best, y'know
The homeless and the tramps
Looking up with soulful eyes
I'm really quite a scamp

For every beggar on the streets

There's a hired dog like me

Lining his pockets with all yer cash

As you live in penury

If poets wrote doggerel 3: (Keats)

Thou still unravish'd bride of quietness

Thou foster child of silence and slow time

Why on Earth am I talking to a Grecian urn?

I must be losing my mind!

Bob The Begging Dog was inspired by a report that beggars in London were making more money than I was at the time and, along with their fortnightly dole cheques, were doing quite nicely, thank you. I too, have had periods when I was out of work and enjoyed the pleasure of looking at the fascinating opportunities placed on little cards at the job centre. This is a poem in praise of The Department of Social Security.

Three Cheers For The Good Old DSS

Three cheers for the good old DSS

The Department of Stealth and Obscurity

The department that says,

"We couldn't care less"

And offers such great opportunity

From stacking of shelves

To waiting on tables

And other such jobs

For the fit and the able

Cashier at Tesco's

Well, it isn't for me

And it's not the best use

Of my honours degree

Haven't you anything
That's more up my street?
Like research assistant
That would be neat

Market research?
Yes, that will do
"Report to this office
Tomorrow at two"

So, now here I stand
With clipboard in hand
Asking which of these toothpastes
Is your favourite brand?

Three cheers for the good old DSS
The Department of Stealth and Obscurity
The department that says,
"We couldn't care less"
And offers such great opportunity

I'm going to get you to cast your minds back to the summer of 2002. World Cup fever was upon us, at least until we were knocked out in the quarter finals by Brazil. With the newspapers full of football, it was hard for any other minor event, say, one's Golden Jubilee, to get a look in. This, I imagine, is what was running through The Queen's mind.

But Will The Peasants Come?

One`s been on the throne for fifty years
One would think they`d make a fuss
But nobody seems that interested
It`s enough to make One cuss

One still believes One`s popular
Although One`s family lets One down
A drunken grandson springs to mind
And of course, One married a clown

The people lead such busy lives
Will they have time, for me?
Or are there more important things
Than Blessed Monarchy?

One`s up against the Football
And World Cup fever`s growing
So will they be chanting Elizabeth
Or more likely, Michael Owen?

It would be nice to see a few streamers
A party or two perhaps
This may be one last chance you see
Should the monarchy collapse

For the times they are a-changing
In this once proud island nation
And there`ll be no royal festivals
When One becomes a federation

And so One sends out party packs
And hopes that something is done
One would like a festive jubilee
But will the peasants come?

If poets wrote doggerel 4: (Browning)

Oh, to be in England

Now that April's here

That overcrowded island

Of rain, and flat, warm beer

It was about this time, or maybe a little earlier, that the village pubs were really beginning to struggle. With the introduction of the brethalyser in the 70s and the draconian anti-smoking legislation of the 80s and 90s, no longer could the village squire motor down to the village ale house for a quiet smoke and a drink. And neither could anyone else. Nowadays you are hard pressed to find a traditional village inn. They're either gastropubs or they've disappeared altogether but at the turn of the millennium they were trying all sorts of things to stay in business, particularly diversification.

The Rose & Crown Shopping Experience (plc)

I walked into the pub today

To buy a pound of sprouts

And met the elderly vicar's wife

Gaily trotting out

"I only went in for stamps," she said

By way of apology

But then I stayed for a sherry

Well maybe two or three."

Our village pub, that bastion

Of carefree inebriation

Is now the village everything
Thanks to diversification

We used to be a sober bunch
A fine, upstanding lot
But now we`re always in the pub
Every one of us a sot

Through the door marked public bar and past the
nearly new bazaar;

The automotive parts display; The local meeting
of AA

I found the landlord in the rear:

"Ice cream? Videos? Turkish rugs? Pile cream?
Prescription drugs?

Groceries? A joint of meat? Stereo? Reclining
seat?

Or maybe just a beer?"

"I`ll have a quick one, as you ask,

I`m meant to be grocery shopping

I`ll have a pint of Post Office Ale

But mind, I won`t be stopping."

A commotion in the other bar
Then caused us some distress
As the local health and fitness champ
Had a cardiac arrest.

"It`s Mr. Jones, he`s dead," they said,
Now what are we to do?"
"Don`t worry," said the landlord,
"I`m the undertaker too."

And that`s how life is nowadays
In villages in The Shires
The pub is there for everything
To rent or buy or hire

But somehow it`s not quite the same
Now it`s part of the daily grind,
The pub was somewhere just to drink
And gradually unwind.

The clock was reading half past two
When I eventually staggered out
And then I staggered in again
I`d forgotten the bloody sprouts.

While we're on the subject of licensed premises, I've travelled extensively in Europe and visited many hostelries of one kind or another. My tipple of choice, on a warm, sunny evening, sitting on a terrace in some country or other, was a Gordon's gin and tonic. But, for a period in the earlier part of this millennium, you couldn't get the stuff for love nor money, nor gin of any description for that matter. Taking pen in hand, I wrote to Messrs. Gordon as follows.

Whatever Happened to Gordon's Gin?

Whatever happened to Gordon's Gin?

It doesn't seem to matter which country I'm in,

I order a Gordon's

The waiter comes back

"We have whisky and vodka,

It is gin that we lack".

En France "Non monsieur,

We do not sell gin.

We have pastis or cognac."

My patience grew thin

Even in Holland
Where gin was invented
The lack of the stuff
Quite drove me demented

Im Deutschland "Nicht haben"
Was the standard reply
"was ist das Gordon"s?"
I was ready to cry.

And finally, stin Hellas
Where they only speak Greek
A man could die of thirst
If it's gin that he seeks.

So where is the Gordon's
Outside the UK?
Or do you not sell it
In Europe these days?

I hope that this shortage

Is just a temporary blip

And your marketing department

Is not losing its grip

Because I love my Gordon's

With tonic and ice

And when I can't get it

Well. It's not very nice

So please reassure me

That things are on track

And there'll be Gordon's on tap

Next time I come back

Unfortunately, I seem to have lost their reply in the intervening years, but I don't recall getting a case of gin by way of recompense. I don't know if the situation has improved, as I no longer drink G + T, but hopefully it has for those of you who do.

If poets wrote doggerel 5: (J. Milton Hayes)

There's a one-eyed yellow idol

To the north of Kathmandu

But what the hell he's doing there

I haven't got a clue

And now we turn to the world of parenting, something thus far, I have managed to avoid. I do have plenty of friends who have children, however, and I've seen what they can do to you. Take this friend of mine and her eight year old daughter.

Life Drawing Class

"Mum, Mum, what can I draw?"

Asked Amy, sprawled out on the living room floor,

"Daffodils, fields and plenty of trees?

"But Mum, I've done that before."

"How about mountains with eagles on high?"

I called, whilst stuffing the washing machine,

"But Mum, you know I can't really draw those,

Think of an easier thing."

"Well, how about, a nice bowl of fruit?

With strawberries, pears and some cherries?"

"I could do," said Amy, thoughtfully,

"But I'm not very good at the berries."

The mobile is ringing, the microwave's pinging
And the Dyson is lying in wait
How can I be expected, to contemplate art,
With the mind of a child of eight?

"You think of something, I'm busy right now,
Think of something that's terribly clever,"
"But I can't," whined Amy, "My mind is a blank
And I can't think of anything.....ever."

"Mum, Mum, what can I draw?"
"Amy, don't nag me to death."
"You draw something Mum, that would be fun."
"ME????   I haven't got time to draw breath!"

Where is the time that my Mum used to find?
She wasn't rushing from crisis to crisis
But life was simpler in my Mother's day
There were no labour saving devices.

What will it be like in twenty years' time,
When Amy has kids of her own?
Draw courage my girl, that's my advice
You'll need it to run your own home.

For sixteen years, I lived on the idyllic island of Crete in the Mediterranean, where I studied and documented the flora and fauna of the eastern province of Lasithi. One of my favourite little animals around the house was the gecko. All geckos were named Gordon, just as all lizards were named Lizzie. Here's a poem for Gordons everywhere.

Gordon The Gecko

Gordon lives in a crack in the wall

He's two inches long and he's not very tall

Gordon lives in a crack in the wall

And he mainly comes out at night

Gordon leaves his crack in the wall

Just after dark, when the sun has gone down

He sits and he gulps and he looks all around

Then he makes his way into the light

Gordon sits above the door by the light

And there he'll sit for most of the night

Waiting for the moths to alight

And then he eats them all

Then before the morning comes

Gordon leaves with his full tum-tum

He pauses by the geranium

And goes back to his crack in the wall

Gordon lives in a crack in the wall

He's two inches long and he's not very tall

Gordon lives in a crack in the wall

And he mainly comes out at night

If poets wrote doggerel 6: (Blake)

Tyger Tyger, burning bright

In the forests of the night

Tell me friend before you die

Which bas*ard set your tail alight?

I recently acquired my first ever mobile phone, a present from my sister who assured me that I couldn't possibly live in England without one. It is a smartphone. It's certainly smarter than me. I feed it money every month, put it to bed lovingly on its charger every night, and attend to it every time it pings, burbles or cries. Leastways, I think it's a phone – on reflection, it may be a Tamagotchi.

Mobile Madness

The scientists are testing

Mobile phones on worms

To see how it affects their genes

And if the worms will turn

The result of their experiments

Will doubtless clearly show

That mobile phones are dangerous

And conclude that they must go

But the tests will be misleading

For what causes worms to ail

Isn`t microwave radiation

It`s constant telephone sales

In every town around the country, you will find a Writers' Circle. A hotch-potch of wannabe writers and poets who gather together, in church halls and libraries, on a wet weekday evening, with the sole purpose of inflicting their scribblings on one another. I used to be the chairman of one of these desperate societies and, to relieve the tedium, we used to inject a quick writing exercise. The idea was, to write a short story or poem in ten minutes, on a given theme. This is the result of one of those exercises where the given theme was 'Joy'.

Incredible Joy

My mother-in-law is eighty-four

An adventurous soul is she

She was bungee jumping at eighty-two

And snorkelling at eighty-three

"What do you want for your Birthday, Joy?"

We asked, with some trepidation

Of this hyperactive O.A.P.

With a vivid imagination

"I want to try hang-gliding this year"

She said, without turning a hair

Which is why we're stood here, on this cliff

Whilst Joy is in the air.

If poets wrote doggerel 7: (Carroll)

T'was brillig when the slithy toves
Did gyre and gimble in the wabe
Pass me a spliff, Alice dear
They're over there by the astrolabe

This bit of nonsense came about whilst watching a military tattoo. The pounding drums suggested the rhythm and the military occasion provided the context. It's about a military gentleman in a retirement home.

The Wandering Albert Ross

I'm Albert Ross of the S.A.S

A para through and through

I can beat the rest 'cause I'm the best

Even though I'm ninety-two

They've got me here in a high-backed chair

Where I sit throughout the day

But they don't know that I plan to go

And escape to Mandalay

I've got my maps and I've got my torch

In the locker by my bed

And an old ruck-sack and some Cherry Black

Which I've stashed in an outside shed

Tonight I'll make my final break
When Nurse Smith has done her rounds
I'll be out through the back and along the track
To the edge of the hospital grounds

They won't catch me 'cause I'm trained, you see
In tactical evasion
I've an apple or two and some Irn Bru
To ward off night starvation

Tonight's the night, they've turned off the light
And It's nearing zero hour
At half past two Nurse goes to the loo
And I start my escape from "The Tower"

Code word red, I'm out of bed
I've never felt leaner or trimmer
Then Abort! Abort! The plan's cut short
Some b*st*rd's nicked me Zimmer

Nurse Smith returns and quickly learns

I'm out of my normal position

She tucks me in with a wicked grin

And threatens me with the physician

But I'm Albert Ross of the S.A.S.

And although the Fates have conspired

I'll try again tomorrow night

When I'm feeling a little less tired

"Albert's wandering again"

I hear as Morpheus claims me

It's changing of the guard on Sunset Ward

I'll escape tomorrow………maybe

In 2020, I moved from Crete in the Mediterranean to Cockermouth in Cumbria. I soon came to realise that I would never be Cockermouth's most famous poet when I discovered that William Wordsworth was born here. Whether his poetry really reflected this idyllic county is open to debate. Here is what I believe he would have written, if he were being more honest:

If poets wrote doggerel 8: Wordsworth

I wandered lonely as a cloud

And then another joined with me

Quite soon there was a gang of us

And we all rained down

Incessantly

Thank you for buying this book and I hope that it raised a smile or two. You can find more of my books on Amazon at www.amazon.co.uk/Steve-Daniels/e/B081Z8FNK5

Or follow me at https://stevesnatureplus541301924.wordpress.com/

Printed in Great Britain
by Amazon

70902321R00031